MARTHA SPEAKS™

Martha Camps Out

MARTHA HABLA
Martha va de campamento

Adaptation by Karen Barss
Based on a TV series teleplay written by Melissa Stephenson and Raye Lankford

Adaptado por Karen Barss. Basado en un guión para televisión
escrito por Melissa Stephenson y Raye Lankford

Based on the characters created by Susan Meddaugh
Basado en los personajes creados por Susan Meddaugh

HOUGHTON MIFFLIN HARCOURT
Boston • New York • 2011

Ages: 5–7 | Grades: 2 | Guided Reading Level: K | Reading Recovery Level: 18
Edad: 5 a 7 años | Grado: 2.ª | Nivel de lectura guiada: K | Nivel de "Reading Recovery": 18

For information about permission to reproduce selections from this book, write to Permissions,
Houghton Mifflin Harcourt Publishing Company, 215 Park Avenue South, New York, New York 10003.

Library of Congress Cataloging-in-Publication Data is on file.
ISBN 978-0-547-55619-2 pb | ISBN 978-0-547-55618-5 hc | ISBN 978-0-547-55795-3 bilingual
Design by Rachel Newborn
www.hmhbooks.com | www.marthathetalkingdog.com

Alice and Helen are Junior Gophers.
Mrs. Clusky is their group leader.
She is taking the two girls camping.

Alicia y Helena son Ardillas Menores. La señora Clusky es
la líder de su grupo. Va a llevar a las niñas de campamento.

Mrs. Clusky says, "Alice and Helen want to earn merit badges."
"Good luck!" the group says.

La señora Clusky dice: —Alicia y Helena quieren ganar su insignia al mérito.
—¡Buena suerte! —dicen sus compañeras.

Alice and Helen pack for the trip to Flea Island.
"I love the outdoors," says Alice. "This is going
to be so much fun!"

Alicia y Helena empacan sus cosas para el viaje. Van a
acampar en la Isla Pulgosa. —Me encanta el aire libre
—dice Alicia—. ¡Nos vamos a divertir muchísimo!

But Alice's brother does not agree.
"You guys are *going camping?*" Ronald asks.
"I would not camp with Big Minnie around."

Pero el hermano de Alicia no está de acuerdo.
—¿Realmente planean *ir de campamento*? —pregunta Ronald—.
Yo no iría de campamento con Gran Mini paseándose por ahí.

"Cut it out, Ronald. You can't scare us," Alice says.
"If it were me," Ronald replies, "I'd be really afraid."

—Deja el fastidio, Ronald —le dice Alicia—. No nos vas a asustar.
—Si fuera yo —responde Ronald—, tendría mucho miedo.

"Who's Big Minnie?" Martha asks.
"Oh, just some monster," Alice says.
"MONSTER!" Martha cries.
"There's no such thing as monsters," Helen says.

—¿Quién es Gran Mini? —pregunta Martha.
—Oh, sólo es un monstruo —le dice Alicia.
—¡UN MONSTRUO! —exclama Martha.
—Los monstruos no existen —le dice Helena.

7

Ronald bikes off.
"Ronald, wait!" calls Martha. "Tell me about Big Minni
Ronald stops. "Some say she isn't real, but she is."

Ronald se aleja pedaleando.
—Espera, Ronald —le dice Martha—. Cuéntame sobre Gran M
Ronald se detiene. —Algunos dicen que no existe, pero es rea

"She only comes out at night," Ronald says.
He uses a spooky voice.
"When the moon is full, she
howls like this:

—Solamente sale de noche —dice Ronald.
Habla con voz aterradora. —Cuando hay luna llena, aúlla así:

Aaaaaaaaaaauuuuuuuuuuuuuuu."

That night, Martha is worried. "If you are going camping," she says to Helen, "I am going with you. I have to protect you!"

Esa noche, Martha está preocupada. —Si vas a ir de campamento —le dice a Helena—, yo iré contigo. ¡Tengo que protegerte!

The next morning is sunny and clear.
The girls, Mrs. Clusky, and the dogs paddle to
Flea Island.

La mañana siguiente amanece clara y soleada.
Las dos niñas, la señora Clusky y los perros reman hacia
Isla Pulgosa.

They work together to set up camp.
They eat around the campfire.

Trabajan en equipo para instalar el campamento.
Luego, comen alrededor de la hoguera.

They prepare for bed. No monsters lurking here!

Se preparan para ir a dormir.
¡No hay ningún monstruo acechando!

Everybody is asleep except Martha and Skits.
They guard the tents. "No sign of Big Minnie,"
Martha says. "I guess we can go to bed."
But just then—

Todos duermen, excepto Martha y Skits. Vigilan las tienda
—No hay rastros de Gran Mini —dice Martha—.
Creo que podemos ir a dormir.
Pero en ese mismo instante...

AAAAA

"I won't tell anyone you are real," says Martha. "I promise."

—No le diré a nadie que eres real —dice Martha—. Te lo prometo.

Martha and Skits jump into the tent.
"It's Big Minnie!" Martha yelps.
"Ronald did her howl for me, just like that!"

Martha y Skits entran a la tienda de un salto.
—¡Es Gran Mini! —ladra Martha—. ¡Ronald imitó su aullido
y el que oímos suena igual!

Alice stands up. "Wait a minute. Ronald howled just like that?"

Alicia se levanta y dice:
—Un momento. ¿Aulló Ronald de la misma manera?

Ronald hides in the woods.

He laughs as he plays his recording.

Ronald está escondido en el bosque.

Se ríe mientras hace sonar la grabación.

Then he hears something in the bushes. What is it?
"Oh, no! It's Big Minnie! She's real!" he shouts.

De repente, escucha algo entre los arbustos.
¿Qué podrá ser?
—¡Oh, no! ¡Es Gran Mini! —grita Ronald—. ¡Es real!

Ronald panics. He runs away.
The girls watch him jump into the lake and swim hom

Ronald se aterroriza. Sale huyendo.
Las niñas lo ven saltar al lago y nadar de regreso a casa.

"That will show him," Alice says, laughing.
"Now let's go back to bed."

—Eso le servirá de lección —dice Alicia riendo—.
Ahora volvamos a dormir.

Back in the tent, a sound wakes Martha.
She peeks outside.
"Hey," Martha whispers, "keep it down—!"
She looks up. Way up.

De vuelta en la tienda, un ruido despierta a Martha.
Ella echa una miradita hacia afuera.
—Oye —susurra Martha—, ¡no hagas tanto ruido...!
Martha mira hacia arriba. Muy arriba.

But Big Minnie purrs softly.
And Martha smiles.
"Hello, Big Minnie," she says,
quietly. "Don't worry. Your secret
is safe with me."

Pero Gran Mini ronronea suavemente.
Martha sonríe.
—Hola, Gran Mini —le dice en voz baja—.
No te preocupes. Tu secreto está seguro
conmigo.